This book belongs to

Bluebell Glade

Dandelion Dell

Heart of Misty Woo

Hawthorn Hedgerows

How many Fairy Animals books have you collected?

- ❀ Chloe the Kitten
- ❀ Bella the Bunny
- ❀ Paddy the Puppy
- ❀ Mia the Mouse
- ✓ Poppy the Pony
- ❀ Hailey the Hedgehog

And there are more magical adventures coming very soon!

Fairy Animals

of Misty Wood

Poppy the Pony

Lily Small

Henry Holt and Company
New York

With special thanks to Thea Bennett

Henry Holt and Company, LLC
Publishers since 1866
175 Fifth Avenue
New York, New York 10010
mackids.com

First published in the United States in 2016 by Henry Holt and Company, LLC.
Originally published in Great Britain in 2014 by Egmont UK Limited.

Library of Congress Cataloging-in-Publication Data
Names: Small, Lily, author.
Title: Poppy the Pony / Lily Small.
Description: First American edition. | New York : Henry Holt and Company, 2016. |
Series: Fairy animals of Misty Wood | Originally published in Great Britain in 2014 by
Egmont Books Ltd. | Summary: "Poppy the Pony is very shy. She loves soaring through
Misty Wood, but she's too scared to talk to any of the other fairy animals. One day a
thunderstorm comes, and Poppy discovers she is braver than she ever knew. Includes
activities"—Provided by publisher.
Identifiers: LCCN 2016001534 (print) | LCCN 2016027193 (ebook) | ISBN 9781627797344
(paperback) | ISBN 9781627797375 (Ebook)
Subjects: | CYAC: Fairies—Fiction. | Ponies—Fiction. | Animals—Fiction. | Bashfulness—
Fiction. | Friendship—Fiction. | BISAC: JUVENILE FICTION / Fantasy & Magic. |
JUVENILE FICTION / Social Issues / Friendship.
Classification: LCC PZ7.S6385 Po 2016 (print) | LCC PZ7.S6385 (ebook) |
DDC [Fic]—dc23
LC record available at https://lccn.loc.gov/2016001534

Our books may be purchased in bulk for promotional, educational, or business use.
Please contact your local bookseller or the Macmillan Corporate
and Premium Sales Department at (800) 221-7945 ext. 5442
or by e-mail at MacmillanSpecialMarkets@macmillan.com.

First American Edition—2016
Printed in the United States of America by
LSC Communications, Harrisonburg, Virginia

5 7 9 10 8 6

Contents

CHAPTER ONE

Poppy Needs a Friend

It was a lovely bright morning in Misty Wood. On top of Sundown Hill, a little pony called Poppy was grazing beside her mom.

POPPY THE PONY

Sundown Hill was the sunniest place in the whole wood. The yellow primroses that grew there shone like sunbeams, and there was plenty of lush green grass, too. Poppy liked the grass very much.

"Yum, yum!" she whinnied as she nibbled the juicy stems. She was nearly full now, but the grass was so tasty she couldn't stop eating.

"That's right, Poppy!" neighed her mom. "We've got lots of work

3

to do today, so you need a big breakfast."

Poppy was a Petal Pony— one of the fairy animals of Misty Wood. Her gleaming coat was the same pale yellow as the primroses and her silky mane and tail were as white as swan feathers. It was the Petal Ponies' special job to swish their glossy tails and waft the beautiful scent of the flowers through the wood. The sweet smells

made all the other animals feel
happy.

"*Woof, woof!*" Loud barking
rang out across the hill.

Poppy stopped chewing and
turned to see who it was.

"Let's have a race!" a voice
called. "I bet I win. *Woof!*"

Poppy heard the patter of
paws on the ground. Lots of paws!
Her long legs started to tremble
as a pack of Pollen Puppies came

5

scampering through the tall grass.

"*Woof!*" they barked as they charged along with their tails wagging. "Hello, Petal Pony. *Woof, woof!*"

But instead of answering, all Poppy could think was *Help!*

You see, Poppy was a very shy pony, and she found it hard to talk to fairy animals she didn't know. Quick as a flash, she unfurled her sky-blue wings

and flew behind her mom to hide.

"Hey, Petal Pony!" barked one of the puppies. "Where did you go?" He peeped through the silky fronds of Poppy's mom's long tail. When he saw Poppy hiding, he trotted around to speak to her.

"There you are," he said with a grin. "We're having a race to Honeydew Meadow. Would you like to come with us?"

Poppy shook her head.

POPPY THE PONY

"Why don't you, Poppy?" said her mom. "You're really good at galloping."

"Yes, you could win the race," barked the puppy. "Come on!"

Poppy hid her face in her long white mane. She felt so shy, she didn't know what to do.

Poppy's mom looked at her kindly. "It'll be fun," she said.

Poppy thought for a moment. Her legs were a lot longer than a

puppy's. And she did love to gallop fast. . . .

"Poppy?" Her mom gave her a nudge with her velvety nose. "What do you say?"

Poppy took a deep breath. She wanted to say, "Yes, please. I'd love to!" But her throat went tight and all that came out was a little snuffling noise that sounded like: "*Hm-hm-hm.*"

The puppy wagged his tail.

"What did you say? Are you coming?"

Poppy hung her head. She was so embarrassed she felt hot all over.

Poppy's mom looked at her, waiting for her to say something, but Poppy's voice had completely disappeared.

"Maybe not today," Poppy's mom told the puppy. "But thank you very much for asking."

"That's okay! Poppy can play

11

anytime." The puppy waved a paw at Poppy to say good-bye. "Come on, puppies, let's go!"

The puppies scampered away over the hill, barking happily.

"I wish I could have gone

with them," Poppy sighed. "But I'm so shy I can't even speak to anybody."

Her mom nuzzled her neck. "You have to try to be a bit braver, Poppy. How will the other animals know that you want to be friends if you don't talk to them?" She lifted her head and gazed down the hill at the rest of Misty Wood. "Never mind now—it's time to start work," she said. "The sun's shining

and all the flowers are blooming."

Poppy's face brightened. She loved swishing the lovely flower smells around the wood.

Her mom looked thoughtful for a second. "Why don't we split up and go to different places today?" she said. "I'll go to Bluebell Glade. You could start at Heather Hill. There'll be lots of gorgeous heather blossoms there."

"I'd rather be with you,"

14

Poppy said, her tail drooping. She'd never gone without her mom before.

"You'll be fine," her mom told her gently. "And maybe other fairy animals will come and talk to you. You might make a friend."

"Maybe," said Poppy, but she didn't think so. How could she make a friend if all she managed to say was *hm-hm-hm*?

"Just give it a try!" her mom said. "Have a lovely day and I'll see

15

you at supper." She nuzzled Poppy with her nose and then galloped off a little way before opening her wings and soaring into the sky.

Poppy felt a bit lonely, left behind on Sundown Hill. But the sun was shining and she had lots of work to do, so she shook out her white mane, fluttered her wings, and headed off.

Misty Wood looked beautiful as she flew over it. When she arrived

at Heather Hill, she heard a loud buzzing. Hundreds of bumblebees were hovering over the purple heather flowers.

Poppy landed in a quiet spot at the side of the hill and began flicking her snowy-white tail over the flowers. A wonderful sweet smell like honey filled the air.

"*Mmmmm!*" droned the bumblebees. They flew up and began swirling in a huge cloud.

Then they zoomed down to collect
pollen, buzzing even more loudly.

Poppy smiled as she listened.
The bees sounded really happy,
and it was all because of her!

It was time to move on and
find some more flowers.

Poppy cantered down Heather
Hill and into the trees. They formed
a beautiful green archway for her
to run through. Thin fingers of
sunlight beamed through the leaves

POPPY NEEDS A FRIEND

above her, making a pretty golden pattern on the floor.

Poppy felt very content as she raced along. But then, just as she reached a clearing, she saw three large fairy animals with stripy faces and silver wings.

Bark Badgers! Poppy skidded to a halt. They mustn't see her, or they might want to come over and talk. Luckily, she spotted a big honeysuckle bush that she could

20

hide behind. She trotted over to it as quietly as she could.

Poppy peeped through the leaves. The badgers were busy doing their special job, decorating the tree bark.

Poppy watched as one badger scraped his claws over the bark, making a flowing line that looked just like a pony's tail. Another was scratching swirly shapes that made Poppy think of a rushing stream.

21

The smallest badger was making a
circle with lots of marks inside. When
he'd finished, it looked as if a face
was smiling out from the tree trunk.

That's so clever! thought Poppy.
She noticed that the honeysuckle

bush she was hiding behind was
covered in white flowers with long
yellow stems. She sniffed. The
flowers smelled so lovely—even
sweeter than the heather blossoms.
Careful not to make a sound, she

slowly swung her tail back and forth and the scent began to drift toward the badgers. The smallest one looked around.

"Mmmm," he murmured, "something smells nice!"

Poppy stopped swishing her tail and kept very still. After a minute, the badger turned back to his tree trunk and began to draw a new pattern with his claws.

"Phew!" Poppy breathed a

24

sigh of relief. He hadn't seen her.

The badgers smiled as they sniffed the honeysuckle perfume. One by one, they began carving beautiful pictures of flowers on their trees. They looked so happy. Poppy's work was done.

She started creeping away from the clearing . . . but the smallest badger looked around again. And this time he spotted her!

"Hello," he called, twirling his silver whiskers in greeting.

Poppy wanted to hide, but she was so shy she couldn't move an inch.

The badger smiled. "You're a Petal Pony."

Poppy nodded. She tried to say something, but nothing came out. It was as if all the words inside her had run away.

"Thank you for making

everything smell so good," the badger said.

Poppy swallowed. She *had* to say something!

"You're welcome," she whispered very quietly.

The badger waited, but Poppy couldn't say anything else.

"Well—thanks again," he said with a friendly wave of his paw, and he turned back to his friends.

Poppy's head fell. The three

badgers were having so much fun, chatting and laughing as they made their beautiful patterns. If only she could go and join in.

"I'll never, ever be able to make a friend," she whispered to herself. A silvery tear ran down her primrose cheek and dripped off the end of her velvety nose.

POPPY NEEDS A FRIEND

CHAPTER TWO

The Bluebirds' Song

Poppy shook the tears from her
eyes and began to trot through the
bright green ferns that grew
in clusters beneath the trees.

She couldn't keep feeling sad—she had to find some more flowers. Suddenly, she spotted something ahead. It looked like a huge mirror, shining brightly on the ground.

"Moonshine Pond!" Poppy neighed. "And it's daytime, so the Moonbeam Moles will all be fast asleep. At least I won't have to worry about bumping into any of them."

The Moonbeam Moles lived in burrows on the banks of the pond.

Their special job was to catch moonbeams and place them in the water to make it glow like a beautiful pearl. Of course, the moles could only collect moonbeams after dark, so they woke up at night and went to bed during the day. Right now they would all be tucked in, fast asleep in their burrows.

Poppy cantered up to the pond. It was very quiet there. The only thing that moved was Poppy's

32

reflection. Her yellow coat and long white mane looked pretty in the gleaming water.

Not far from the pond, Poppy could see little heaps of earth that marked the entrances to the moles' burrows. She went over and bent her head to see if she could hear the moles inside.

A funny grunting and whistling noise was coming up from under the ground.

"*Och, och, phweee . . .*"

"*Phwee, och, och . . .*"

The moles were snoring! They certainly wouldn't disturb her while she did her work.

Poppy saw some lavender bushes close by. She trotted over and swung her long tail to and fro over the lilac flowers.

"*Aaaah!*" she heard the moles sigh. "*Mmmmm!*" they breathed as the soothing lavender scent reached their sleepy noses, deep underground.

Poppy smiled. Her work at Moonshine Pond was finished. She flicked her wings and soared up

35

through the trees, heading for the
Heart of Misty Wood.

Soon she came to a place
where the trees grew very tall.
Beneath the trees was a grassy
glade, and Poppy drifted toward it.
As she landed, the grass felt as soft
as a cushion under her hooves.

High above in the treetops,
Poppy heard the flutter of wings.
She looked up. Two bluebirds had
landed on a branch.

"*Tweet-tweet*," sang one, flicking his bright blue tail.

"*Cheep-cheep*," replied the other, nodding her little blue head.

Poppy pricked her ears to listen to their lovely song. But they were

so high up it sounded very faint. If only they would come closer.

Then Poppy had an idea. She walked over to a rose bush that was growing at the edge of the glade. She brushed her tail over the velvety pink petals, and a beautiful scent rolled like mist across the glade.

One of the bluebirds looked down, his head tilted to the side.

Poppy swept her tail over the roses again.

"*Twee-ee-eet!*" sang the bluebird
as the perfume drifted up to him.
He leaped off the branch and flew
down to the grass.

"*Chee-ee-eep!*" trilled his mate
as she joined him.

The two birds hopped around
and fluttered their blue wings as
if they were dancing. They hadn't
noticed Poppy.

They like the smell of roses, Poppy
thought with a smile.

There was a rustle at the edge of the glade and a shiny brown nose peeped through a cluster of ferns. A Stardust Squirrel with wings as bright as starshine emerged. Poppy darted behind some trees so he wouldn't see her. But then a voice spoke up on the other side of the nearest tree trunk.

"Ho hum, tiddly-pum! Just look at all these leaves . . ."

Poppy peeped around the tree

trunk. A Hedgerow Hedgehog was rolling around on the ground, collecting dead leaves on her spines.

"*Tweet-tweet! Cheep-cheeep!*" warbled the bluebirds.

"What a lovely song!" the hedgehog sighed. "I think I'll take a break." She sat down to listen. She still had leaves stuck all over her back like a coat.

Who's going to turn up next? thought Poppy. She made herself as

41

small as she could so the hedgehog wouldn't notice her.

"*Tweety-tweet-cheep!*" trilled the bluebirds.

Now Poppy could hear rustling noises all around her. She felt her heart beating fast. There were fairy animals everywhere, making their way into the glade. A herd of Dream Deer trotted past, lifting their graceful heads as they sniffed the roses. Some Bark Badgers

pushed their stripy faces through the ferns to watch the birds. Pollen Puppies, tails wagging, flopped on the ground to listen.

More and more animals arrived. Cobweb Kittens floated down through the air. Moss Mice and Holly Hamsters fluttered out from behind the trees, their tiny wings twinkling.

"Tweeety-tweet! Cheepy-cheep!" sang the bluebirds.

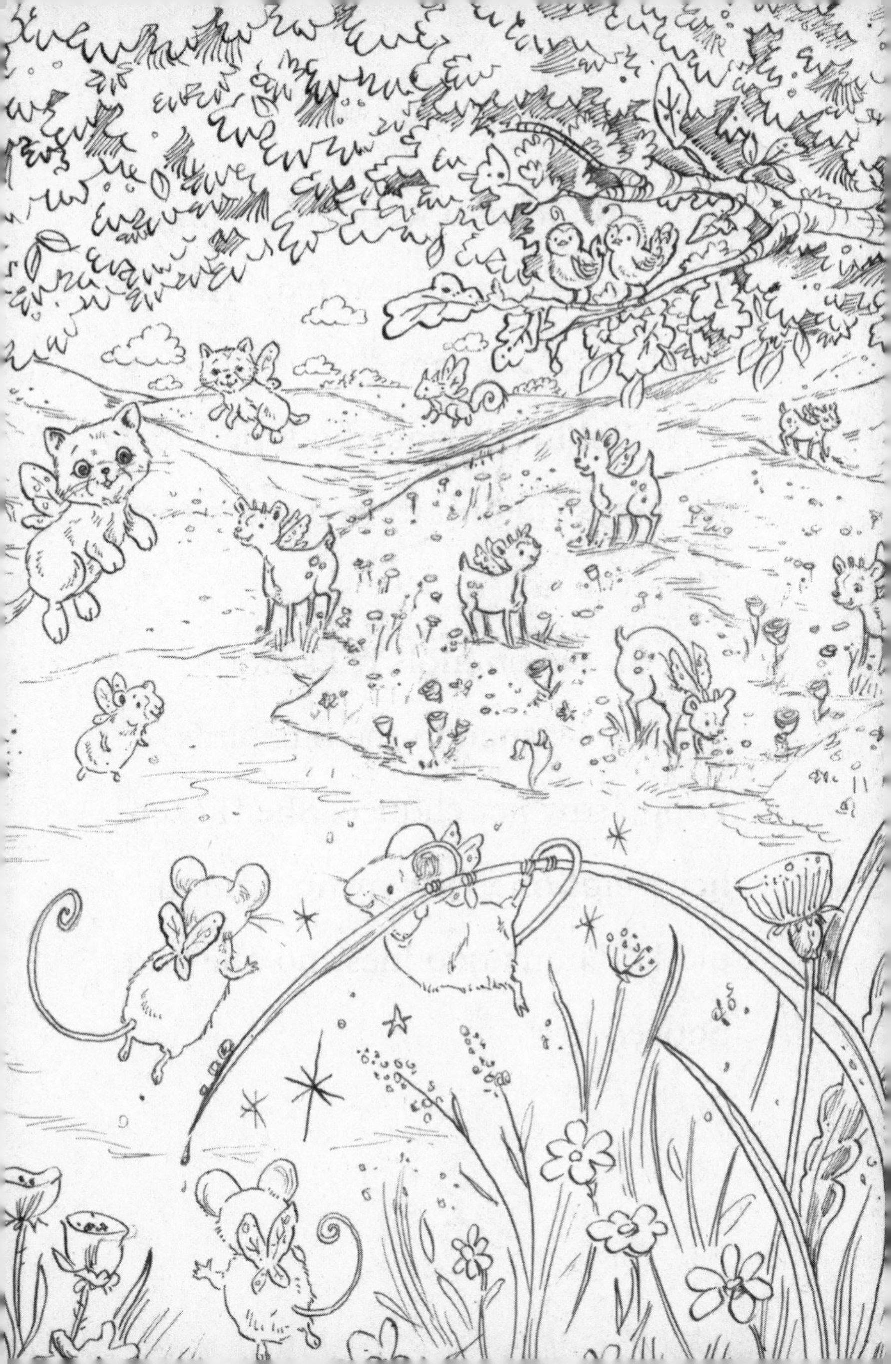

"Ah, what a wonderful song," a Bark Badger murmured. "And it smells so *lovely* here."

"Shhh," squeaked a little Moss Mouse, swinging from a grass stem. "Just listen!"

All the animals fell silent. As they listened to the bluebirds, Poppy saw her chance. She flicked her wings and flew away from the glade. Thank goodness no one had noticed her!

Poppy flew swiftly through the wood. She was just beginning to feel tired when she saw a gnarled old tree with juicy golden pears hanging from its branches. It had been a long time since breakfast and she was feeling very hungry, so she swooped down and landed under the tree.

She was just about to take a bite from one of the fallen pears when she heard a voice from above.

"Help!" the voice squeaked.

Poppy froze. Someone was in the tree and they were calling to her! But what was she going to do?

CHAPTER THREE

Poppy to the Rescue!

Everything went quiet. Poppy was just wondering whether she'd imagined the voice when she heard it again.

"Help!" it cried. "Please help me!"

Poppy was puzzled. She hadn't seen anyone at all when she flew over the pear tree.

"Who are you?" she tried to say, but her voice wasn't working again and all that came out was "*Hm-hm-hm?*"

"I'm stuck!" the voice whimpered. "Please help me."

Whoever it was sounded very scared.

Poppy peered up. A tiny Cobweb Kitten, with fur the color of chocolate, was clinging to a high branch.

51

"Please! I want to get down," the kitten meowed, letting go of the branch and waving her paws at Poppy.

Poppy was amazed. The kitten wasn't holding on—so why hadn't she fallen out of the tree? Then Poppy saw that one of the kitten's golden wings was trapped.

Poppy felt so sorry for the kitten that she forgot all about being shy. "You poor thing," she

52

neighed. "Of course I'll help you get down."

"Oh, thank you!"

"What's your name? And how did you get stuck up there?" Poppy called. Her voice was working perfectly now—she didn't even have to think about it.

The kitten was trembling. "My name's Coco," she meowed. "What's yours?"

"Poppy," Poppy replied.

"Hello, Poppy. I was just on my way to meet my friends for a picnic when I spotted these juicy pears."

Poppy nodded. "They do look delicious."

"I thought they'd be perfect for the picnic," Coco said. "I swooped down to pick one, but then my wing got caught."

Poppy tossed her white mane. Then, with a swirl of her shimmering wings, she flew up

to the branch. But as soon as she landed, Poppy realized she couldn't reach Coco with her nose. There were too many twigs and leaves in the way.

"Please be quick!" Coco pleaded. "My wing is getting sore."

Carefully, Poppy turned and twirled her tail over Coco's wing, twisting it gently until it came free.

Coco leaped off the branch . . . then squealed with fright.

Poppy saw Coco tumbling down! She flapped her wings hard and flew after her. When she was close enough, she flicked out her tail as far as it would go and managed to catch Coco just before she hit the ground.

"Thank you so much!" Coco gasped as Poppy lowered her onto the grass. "My wing isn't working properly. I can't fly."

A tear welled in Coco's eye.

POPPY TO THE RESCUE!

"And if I can't fly, I'll never get to the picnic in time."

The little kitten looked so sad that Poppy didn't stop to think. "I could take you there if you like," she said in a very soft voice.

Coco was so pleased she jumped up and down. "Ouch!" she squeaked as she tried to flutter her wings. "I must remember not to do that. Thank you, Poppy!"

"You're welcome," Poppy said.

Coco was being so bouncy it made Poppy feel shy again, so she didn't say anything else. She wrapped her tail around the kitten and lifted her onto her back.

"Ooh, this is so much fun!" Coco meowed, holding on to Poppy's coat with her paws. "I've always wondered what it must be like to be a Petal Pony—to gallop so fast and fly so high. Now I'm going to find out!"

59

Poppy tossed her head. She couldn't help feeling a little bit proud that Coco might want to be like her. "Let's go!" she neighed.

Coco told Poppy that the picnic was happening near Dewdrop Spring. Poppy set off through the trees at a smooth trot. Soon they came out into Honeydew Meadow.

"Could we go a bit faster?" asked Coco.

"Are you sure?" Poppy said.

"I don't want you to fall off."

"I'll hold on tight, I promise,"
Coco said.

Poppy stretched out her neck

and began to race across the golden flowers.

"Wheeee!" Coco squealed as Poppy leaped over a fallen log. "Woo-hooo!" she whooped as Poppy kicked up her heels and jumped over a hedge.

Poppy's hooves thundered across the golden meadow. When she couldn't gallop any faster, she unfurled her wings and soared into the air.

62

"Oooooh!" Coco meowed.

Poppy felt the little kitten
clinging to her mane as they
floated high over a hill where lots of
green bushes grew.

"Those are the Mulberry
Bushes," Poppy said. "That's where
the Misty Wood Rabbit Warren is."

"We're nearly there, then!"
squeaked Coco. "Dewdrop Spring
runs right by the rabbit warren.
Look, there are my friends!"

63

Poppy glanced down. She could see the silvery thread of Dewdrop Spring winding its way past the warren. Then she saw three fairy animals spreading out a picnic blanket made of moss on the banks of the spring. There was a Bud Bunny, a Moss Mouse, and a Holly Hamster.

Poppy's wings began to tremble. It was okay being with Coco. It was easy talking to just

one little kitten. But what would happen if she had to meet three new fairy animals all at once?

CHAPTER FOUR

Picnic Time!

Poppy's heart pounded as she
glided toward Dewdrop Spring.

"Hey—look at meeee!" Coco
called to her friends down below.

The three fairy animals were very surprised indeed when they looked up and saw Coco on Poppy's back.

"How did you get to ride on a Petal Pony?" squeaked the Moss Mouse.

"That looks like fun!" chuckled the Bud Bunny.

"Come down and start the picnic! I'm starving!" shouted the Holly Hamster, rubbing his furry tummy.

Poppy's blue wings glimmered as she circled in the air, looking for somewhere to land. She felt very shy with all of Coco's friends watching her.

Next to the picnic spot there was a grassy bank covered with bright yellow buttercups. Poppy fluttered down toward it.

"I'll drop you here, Coco," she whinnied. As soon as her hooves touched the ground, she carefully

lifted Coco down with her tail. "I've got to go now," she explained hurriedly. "I've got loads of work to do and—"

But it was too late.

The Bud Bunny came hopping toward them through the buttercups. "Coco—who's your friend?" she asked.

Poppy hid her face in her mane. If only she'd flown away more quickly!

Then the Moss Mouse scampered up, his long whiskers twitching. "Are you all right, Coco?"

"I got stuck in a tree!" Coco explained. "I was trying to pick some pears for our picnic, but my wing got caught. It was horrible." Coco's tail fluffed up like a feather duster at the thought.

"That sounds awful. Oh, look, here comes hungry Harry!" said

the bunny as the Holly Hamster

trotted up on his chubby little legs.

"Who said pears? Did you say

pears?" he said to Coco, puffing

out his cheeks. "I love pears. Did

you bring some?"

Coco shook her head. "No,
I was too scared to pick any.
I thought I'd be stuck up there
forever."

"How did you escape?" asked
the mouse.

"Poppy rescued me," Coco
purred. "She's amazing!" The kitten
twined herself around Poppy's legs,
rubbing them with her soft fur as
she told her friends how the pony
had freed her from the tree.

Coco's friends all looked at Poppy in admiration.

"I'm Max," squeaked the Moss Mouse, standing as tall as he could on his back legs and twirling his whiskers at Poppy.

"I'm Bobbi," said the Bud Bunny, twitching her velvety pink nose.

"And I'm hungry—*starving* hungry!" said Harry.

Poppy looked down at the

buttercups and tried to pretend that she wasn't really there. Her heart was beating so fast, and she felt too hot. If only they would all stop staring at her!

Harry looked longingly over at the picnic blanket. "Let's eat before my tummy gets so empty it starts to cry!" he groaned.

They all turned to the picnic. Poppy was relieved. Finally, she had a chance to escape. She spread

her wings, ready to take off. But just then, Max looked back.

"Don't go!" he cried when he saw her.

Poppy opened her mouth and tried to speak, but all that came out was, "*Hm-hm-hm!*"

Coco padded over and rubbed against Poppy's legs again. "You must come to our picnic," she purred.

"Please stay, Poppy!" Bobbi said.

"If you don't all hurry up, I am going to faint from starvation!" Harry called, sucking his cheeks in as thin as they would go—which wasn't very thin at all.

It was no good. Poppy's voice had disappeared again, and she didn't want to seem rude. All she could do was fold her wings back down and trot after the others to the picnic spot.

The mossy blanket was covered

with conker-shell bowls full of nuts and seeds, bunches of tasty carrots with leafy green tops, and a basket of beautiful rosy apples.

Coco, Bobbi, Max, and Harry settled down and started eating. But Poppy felt much too shy to sit down with them. So she stood behind, shifting nervously from hoof to hoof. She was very glad that they were all too busy enjoying the food to notice her.

If I went back to the buttercup patch, she thought, *I could wave my tail over the flowers to spread the perfume. Everyone would be happy, and they'd forget all about me.*

She was just about to slip away when Coco looked around. "Would you like an apple?" she asked.

Before Poppy could even try to answer, the little kitten came padding over with a shiny red

apple in her mouth. She put it
down in front of Poppy.

Poppy licked the apple, but
she didn't bite into it. If she made

a loud crunching noise, everyone would look at her again.

"Oooh!" squealed Coco suddenly. "What was that?" She wiped at her head with her paw.

Poppy felt a fat drop of water plop onto her mane.

Everyone looked up. The sun had disappeared, and a big black cloud was filling up the sky. It was starting to rain!

"Oh no!" squeaked Max,

holding a carrot over his head as the drops began falling thick and fast. "Our picnic will be ruined!"

83

CHAPTER FIVE

Under the Oak Tree

"I'm getting wet," meowed Coco, shaking raindrops out of her fur.

"Me too," squeaked Max. "We'd better get out of here."

"Never mind about getting wet—what about the food?" Harry cried. He started scampering about, gathering all the food in the middle of the mossy blanket. Then he folded the corners together and tied them tightly in a knot.

"Where can we go?" asked Bobbi, flicking the rain from her floppy ears. "There's no shelter here."

The rain was coming down

really hard now. *At least it will make the flowers grow*, Poppy thought.

But she felt very sorry for the four friends. Their picnic was spoiled and they were going to get soaked. If she was brave enough, maybe she could help . . .

She took a deep breath. "Jump on my back!" she whinnied. As soon as the words burst from her mouth, she felt so shy she had to look down at her hooves.

"Really, Poppy?" said Bobbi, her eyes shining.

"Come on, quick!" said Coco, scampering up Poppy's tail and onto her back.

Bobbi did a giant hop and landed just behind Coco.

Harry and Max fluttered their little wings and floated up to join the others. "Don't forget the food!" Harry shrieked.

"I won't," Poppy said. "Hold

on tight!" She picked up the blanket
bundle with her mouth and started
cantering away from Dewdrop
Spring.

"Wheeee!" squealed Coco.

"Isn't this fun?"

"Bouncing bunnies!" cried

Bobbi. "It's brilliant!"

Poppy's tail streamed behind her as she galloped toward the trees. She knew just where to go. Right in the heart of the wood grew a tall oak tree with wide, leafy branches big enough to cover them all.

As soon as she spotted the tree, she slowed down to a gentle trot.

"This is perfect! We'll be dry here," squeaked Max as Poppy came to a halt.

Poppy carefully placed the blanket of food on the ground under the tree. Max and Harry fluttered down, and Bobbi and Coco both reached the ground in one big leap.

"Thank you, Poppy," said Harry as he untied the blanket with his front teeth. "I was saving the biggest apple for me, but you can have it. You deserve it!"

This time, Poppy was so glad

Coco's friends were happy that she didn't feel shy or embarrassed. She just took a bite out of the juicy apple and kept on crunching until it was all gone. When she'd finished, she noticed that Coco had disappeared.

"Where's Coco?" she asked.

"I'm here!" purred Coco, scampering up to Poppy with a bunch of daisies. "Lie down, Poppy, and shut your eyes—I'm

going to give you a wonderful surprise."

Poppy lay down with her legs folded underneath her. She closed her eyes. She could feel Coco playing with her mane—it was lovely. Her whole body relaxed.

Finally, Coco tapped Poppy on the nose. "Okay—ready!"

When Poppy opened her eyes, she saw that Coco had woven a daisy chain into her mane. The

93

little flowers looked like yellow and white jewels.

"Thank you!" she whinnied.

"It's so pretty!"

"Thank *you*," replied Coco.

"You saved us from getting soaking wet. That rain is heavy—listen."

Poppy pricked her ears. *Pit-a-pat, pit-a-pat* went the raindrops as they sploshed on the leaves of the oak tree.

Suddenly, there was a loud *CRACK!* from high up in the sky.

"Uh-oh!" Bobbi cried. "A thunderstorm!"

"Help!" squealed Harry. He covered his ears with his paws.

"I'm scared," whispered Max as another *CRACK!* echoed through the sky.

"It's all right," said Poppy. "Hide under my mane, you two little ones. You'll be safe there."

"Wh-wh-what about all the f-f-f-food?" Harry stammered as he and Max snuggled under Poppy's mane. "What if it gets struck by lightning?"

"It won't," Poppy said calmly

as she gathered the remains of the picnic toward her with her tail. Coco and Bobbi cuddled up next to her tummy. Poppy felt very brave and strong as she swooshed her tail around to hug them close.

BOOM! went the thunder. Poppy could feel Max and Harry trembling. Coco and Bobbi were shivering, too. What could she do to make them forget about the thunder? Then she had an idea.

She'd have to be very brave indeed,

but maybe it would work. . . .

Poppy took a deep breath.

"Shall I tell you a story?" she

asked. She gave a small sigh of
relief. Her voice was still working!

"Yes, please!" said Bobbi.

Poppy cleared her throat.
"Once upon a time," she began in
a strong, clear voice, "there was a
baby Petal Pony called Pearl. Her
legs were so wobbly she couldn't
stand up."

"Why were they wobbly?"
asked Max.

"Because she was only one

99

hour old, and she hadn't learned how to walk yet," said Poppy. "It's quite hard to get the hang of walking when your legs are as long as a Petal Pony's."

"I'd be very scared if that was me," Harry said.

"Pearl wasn't *too* scared, because her mom was with her," Poppy said, "and her mom was very nice and kind. 'Come on, Pearl—you can do it,' her mom

said. So Pearl put her front hooves on the ground and pushed until she was halfway up, and . . ."

BOOM! went the thunder. All the animals cowered back against Poppy.

"What happened next?" Coco asked in a shaky voice.

"Pearl pushed and pushed with her hooves, but her legs were still too wobbly. Bump—down she fell again," said Poppy.

101

"Poor little Pearl," said Bobbi. "I hope there's a happy ending for her."

"So do I!" said a gruff voice, and a Bark Badger pushed his stripy face through the bushes.

Then a graceful Dream Deer stepped out from behind the tree. "I'm sure there is," she said in a soft, soothing voice. "But we'll have to hear the rest of the story to find out. . . ."

Now there were rustling noises from all around. Lots of fairy animals were coming under the oak tree to take shelter from the rain. There were Stardust Squirrels and Hedgerow Hedgehogs, Bud Bunnies and Pollen Puppies—and they were all looking at Poppy and waiting for her to continue her story.

There were so many of them that Poppy began to feel a little

103

POPPY THE PONY

shy again. What would she do if
her voice stopped working and she
couldn't tell the rest of the story?

She spotted a patch of pansies
growing from the roots of the oak
tree. She swished her tail softly over
the purple flowers, and a soothing
perfume drifted out.

"Mmm!" sighed Max as he
climbed out from under Poppy's
mane. "That smells nice. I'm not a
bit frightened of the thunder now."

105

All the fairy animals who had gathered around were looking calm and happy, too.

Poppy went on. "Pearl's mom said: 'Come on, Pearl, you can do it,' and she nudged Pearl with her nose. 'I can't!' said Pearl. 'My legs won't work!' 'They will,' said Pearl's mom. 'You've just got to believe.'"

Poppy paused for a moment. She looked around at all the animals. Their eyes shone as they

waited to hear what happened next to baby Pearl. They'd forgotten all about the thunderstorm.

"Pearl stretched out her front legs," Poppy continued. "'I *can* stand up!' she said, and she pushed and she pushed until she was almost up, but then her legs started wobbling again. . . ."

A whisper went up from the animals: "*Come on, baby Pearl! You can do it!*"

107

"Pearl's mom reached out with her nose and she pushed against Pearl's tail so she didn't fall over again—and suddenly, Pearl was standing up!"

"Hooray!" cried the animals.

"Baby Pearl took one wobbly step, and then she took another. Then Pearl's mom trotted away!"

"No!" squeaked Max. "What did Pearl do?"

Poppy smiled at him and

carried on with the story. "'Don't go without me!' Pearl whinnied. And suddenly she found that her legs were working! Faster and faster they went—until she was galloping after her mom! 'I *can* do it!' Pearl neighed as she cantered along at her mom's side. 'Yes, you can,' her mom said. 'And one day, you'll be the fastest Petal Pony in Misty Wood.' The end!" said Poppy.

"Yay!" A big cheer went up from all the animals.

They liked her story! Poppy tossed her head and flicked her long mane with its pretty daisy chain.

And the strangest thing
was that although everyone was
looking at her, Poppy didn't feel the
slightest bit shy.

CHAPTER SIX

Surprise!

Max fluttered his wings and flew beside Poppy's head. "Was that story really about you?" he whispered.

"Yes," Poppy whispered back. "My mom helped me to stand up

when I was a baby. And one day, maybe I'll be the fastest pony in Misty Wood!"

"I bet you will," said Max.

"The rain's stopped," said Coco, looking up at the top of the oak tree. "The storm's over!" The little Cobweb Kitten fluttered her wings and flew back and forth over the ferns. "My wing's healed!" she called. "Your story made me feel better, Poppy!"

Poppy swished her tail and neighed happily. Lots of other animals started coming over to talk to her. Poppy jumped to her feet, but there was nothing to be shy about. Everyone just wanted to be friendly.

"Your mane would make a great bark pattern," said one of the Bark Badgers. "Come and pose for us sometime. Maybe you could tell us another story—and make

114

everything smell lovely and sweet again?"

"Come around and visit us for snacks!" said a Stardust Squirrel. "We've got some tasty hazelnuts!"

"Hazelnuts? Who said hazelnuts?" Harry cried.

"*Woof! Woof!*" barked a Pollen Puppy. "How about a game of chase? Whenever you like, we'll be ready! *Woof!*"

A Dream Deer blinked shyly

at Poppy. "Would you like to come running through the woods with us?" she murmured. "You could spread the flower smells and tell us a story while we go!"

Max's whiskers were twitching again. "I was just thinking," he squeaked. "You might be tired after all that running around and storytelling. Drop by my burrow and we'll make you a big comfy moss cushion to lie on."

"I would love that! Thank you," said Poppy.

Golden shafts of sunlight were shimmering through the branches now. The leaves and ferns of Misty Wood looked so fresh and green. All that was missing was the sweet smell of flowers. The rain had washed it away! It was time for Poppy to get going.

"I'll come and visit you all," Poppy said to her new friends. "And

117

we'll have loads of fun. But first I've got my special job to do. Good-bye for now—and I'll see all of you very soon!"

As the fairy animals called their good-byes, Poppy twirled her blue wings and floated away through the trees. The leafy branches were covered in dazzling raindrops that glinted in the sunlight, and a rainbow twinkled softly in the sky.

SURPRISE!

Poppy glided down and swished her tail over the bluebells and buttercups, roses and lilies, until Misty Wood was filled with the sweetest smells once again. Finally, as the sky was turning pink and the sun began to fade, she galloped back to Sundown Hill.

Her mom was waiting for her, looking worried. "There you are, Poppy!" she neighed. "Did you get caught in the rain?"

Poppy blew on her mom's nose to say hello. "I was fine," she said. "The thunder was very loud, though."

"It was," Poppy's mom said with a shiver. "I was worried about you, all on your own in the storm."

Poppy was about to explain what had happened when there was a flicker of wings close by. It was Max!

"Hello, Poppy," he squeaked as

he fluttered past. "Don't forget to come and get your pony-sized moss cushion!"

Poppy's mom's eyes opened wide with surprise, but before she could say anything, a Bark Badger came trundling through the grass.

"See you soon!" he called to Poppy. "Drop by anytime!"

"Poppy! What's going on?" asked her mom.

Poppy was just about to answer

when a Dream Deer strolled past.
"Can't wait to go running with
you!" the deer called softly.

Then a Pollen Puppy bounced
up. "See you soon for our game
of chase," he yelped, and then
scampered away.

"Well!" Poppy's mom said with
a smile. "You *have* been busy, Poppy.
Very busy indeed!" She nuzzled
Poppy's neck. "And what's this lovely
daisy chain doing in your mane?"

Poppy felt her heart swell as she thought of all the fairy animals she had met that day. Her first-ever friends! There was no need to be shy after all.

"A *friend* made it for me!" Poppy told her mom, who looked as pleased as Poppy felt.

Then Poppy kicked up her heels, neighed with joy, and cantered off to find a tasty patch of grass for her supper.

Turn the page for

lots of fun

Misty Wood

activities!

Picnic Time!

In the story, Poppy's new friends have a delicious picnic with lots of tasty treats for everyone.

What are your favorite things to eat at a picnic? Write them down on the next page.

1. ....
2. ....
3. ....
4. ....
5. ....
6. ....
7. ....
8. ....

Draw the treats from your list on page 129 on the picnic blanket.

Connect the Dots

Follow the numbers and connect all the dots to make a lovely picture from the story.

Start with dot number 1. When you've connected all the dots, try drawing Poppy's new friends around her!

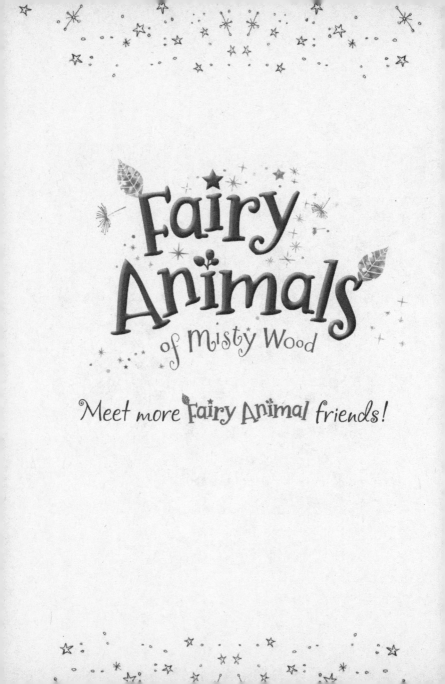

Fairy Animals

of Misty Wood

Meet more Fairy Animal friends!